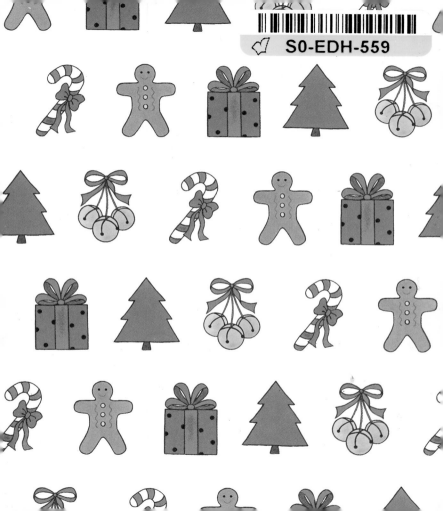

Alex
Xmas 1999

The Nutcracker

Christmas was soon approaching! Clara and her little brother, Fritz, eagerly awaited the presents they hoped to find under the Christmas tree. Clara dreamed of beautiful dolls and Fritz imagined rows and rows of shiny, tin soldiers.

On Christmas Eve, Clara's parents gave a wonderful party. The Christmas tree sparkled and many presents lay beneath it.

The last guest to arrive at the party was Herr Drosselmeyer, Clara's godfather. Everyone loved him. He was a wonderful toymaker and he told marvelous stories. His toys were so life-like, the children wondered if they were actually real!

As soon as Christmas dinner was finished, the children eagerly unwrapped their gifts.

This Christmas, Herr Drosselmeyer brought Clara a very special present...a Nutcracker dressed like a soldier.

"This is my favorite Christmas present!" Clara said with delight.

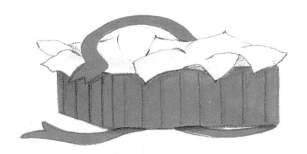

Fritz glared at the Nutcracker and said, "He's ugly!" He grabbed the Nutcracker from Clara, pushed a nut into his mouth, and slammed it shut. Crack! The Nutcracker's jaw was broken!

Almost in tears, Clara picked up the Nutcracker. "He'll be handsome again in the morning," whispered Herr Drosselmeyer as he tied a handkerchief around the Nutcracker's broken jaw.

Late that night,
as the clock struck
midnight...

...Clara tiptoed to the toy room to check on her broken Nutcracker. She was startled – Herr Drosselmeyer was sitting on top of the clock while mice scampered across the floor!

The mice seemed larger than life to Clara, as did Fritz's toy soldiers. Soon, the toy soldiers and the mice were engaged in battle...bugles were blowing and drums were beating!

To Clara's amazement, the Nutcracker came to life, grabbed a sword, and joined the battle. Suddenly, an evil Mouse King wearing a golden crown and carrying a sword, appeared out of the ranks of mice.

As the Mouse King advanced toward the Nutcracker with his sword raised, Clara pulled off her slipper and threw it at the King! The slipper found its target and the Mouse King fell.

All at once, everything vanished and all that remained where the battle had been, was the Nutcracker, who had turned into a handsome prince!

"Come with me, Clara!" said the Nutcracker Prince, as he whisked her away through the Kingdom of Snow. Snowflakes danced and glistened on the trees.

They arrived at the Land of Sweets, where they were greeted by the Sugar Plum Fairy. The Prince told the Fairy how Clara had saved him from the wicked Mouse King. "We must honor this brave girl," said the Sugar Plum Fairy, as she escorted Clara and the Prince to a candy throne.

Ladies from Spain and from Arabia danced in exotic costumes. Clara was enthralled.

Dancers from around the world performed for Clara and the Prince.

Chinese acrobats and swirling Cossacks held Clara's attention. Flowers waltzed with the Sugar Plum Fairy...what a fantasy!

Floating on a soft cloud, Clara waved goodbye to the Land of Sweets, the Sugar Plum Fairy, and the Nutcracker Prince as they faded from her sight.

Clara awoke in the nursery with the Nutcracker doll still in her arms. Was it all just a lovely dream?